Living Lights™
A Faith Story

The Berenstain Bears'
Caring and Sharing
Treasury

5 BOOKS IN 1

ZONDERkidz

By Jan & Mike Berenstain

ZONDERKIDZ

The Berenstain Bears® Caring and Sharing Treasury
Copyright © 2016 by Berenstain Bears, Inc.
Illustrations © 2016 by Berenstain Bears, Inc.

Requests for information should be addressed to:
Zonderkidz, 3900 *Sparks Dr. SE, Grand Rapids, Michigan 49546*

ISBN 978-0-310-75358-2

The Berenstain Bears® Jobs Around Town ISBN 9780310722861 (2011)
The Berenstain Bears® Get Involved ISBN 9780310720904 (2012)
The Berenstain Bears® Love Their Neighbors ISBN 9780310712497 (2009)
The Berenstain Bears® Gossip Gang ISBN 9780310720850 (2011)
The Berenstain Bears® and the Biggest Brag ISBN 9780310734796 (2014)

Editor: Mary Hassinger
Cover and interior design: Diane Mielke

Printed in China

16 17 18 19 20 21 22 23 24 25 26 27 28 /LPC/ 17 16 15 14 13 12 11 10 9 8 7 6 5 4 3 2 1

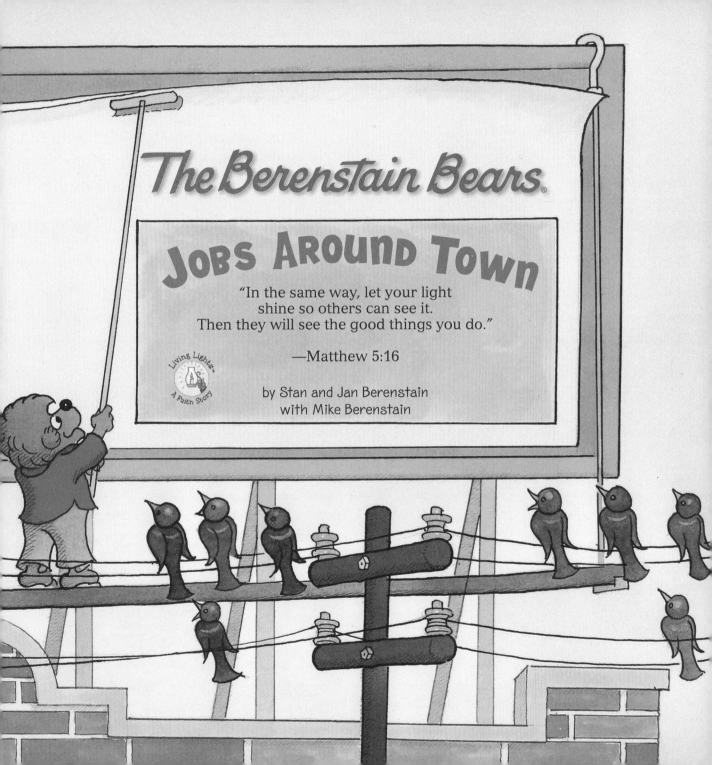

In Bear Country, there are many jobs to be done. Mama takes care of our tree house and family. Papa does chores and makes fine furniture to sell. But there are other jobs too. And if you pick the right job, work will be fun.

Let's take a trip around Bear Country and see what we might be when we grow up.

Some jobs can be exciting. We could fight fires like Firebear Bob.

Or we could be policebears like Officer Marguerite. She tells us when to safely cross the road. If we don't obey, she blows her whistle ...

TWEET

We might be Beartown bus drivers. Or we might learn to drive a delivery truck, an ambulance, or even a cement mixer.

Mama and Papa say God gives everyone a special talent. We can use our talent to do the job that is best for us and help others too.

Some folks are good at fixing things. They might be plumbers, mechanics, carpenters, or watchmakers. Almost everything we use sometimes has to have a fixer!

banana
b-a-n-a-n-a
dinosaur
d-i-n-o-s-a-u-r

It would be fun to be a teacher and teach cubs how to read and write...

or a doctor and help make folks well.

We could have a store and sell good things like honey and bread.

Or we could work in a bank where money is kept safe and sound.

Engineers figure out better ways to build things. We could be engineers and build big bridges here in Bear Country.

Scientists study nature and try to find out about new things.
Maybe we can become scientists and cure diseases!

We could use our God-given talents to build buildings proud and tall.

Or we might be wreckers and tear down old unsafe buildings. That would be cool—POW!

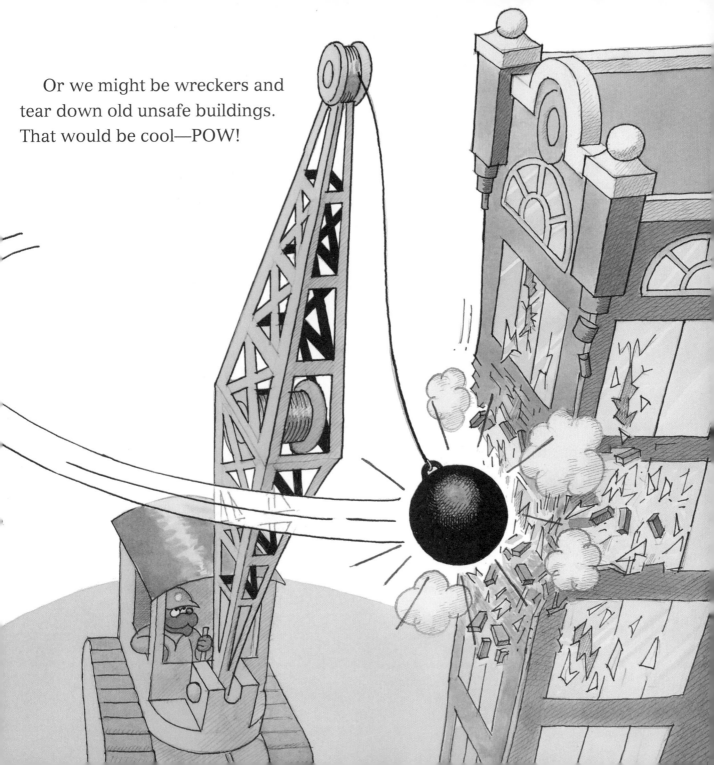

Brother, do you think my God-given talent is to be a singer? I've always loved to sing!

On second thought, I don't think I should. Maybe I don't really have a singing voice.

Don't worry, Sister, our job hunt is not over yet.

There are so many things to do and be. And the choice is up to you.

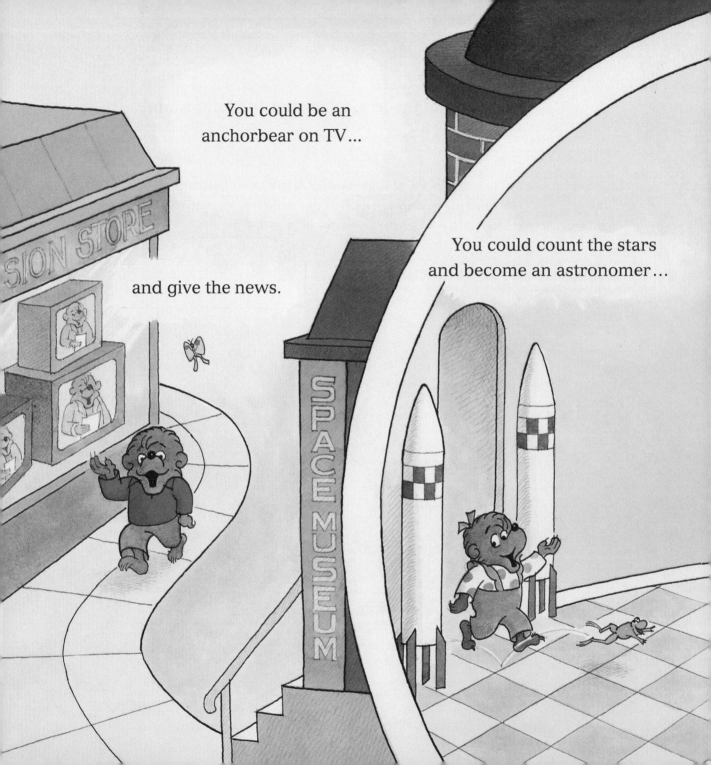

or an astronaut and
visit distant planets
like Jupiter and Mars!

Hey, Sister! Look here. I love computer games. I could work with computers.

But I love Bear Country too. Being an environmentalist and helping stop pollution could be great.

Forest rangers protect the trees by watching out for forest fires.

Or we could become farmers like our good neighbor, Farmer Ben.

Mr. and Mrs. Ben raise champion pigs. We could do that on our farm too. Our champion pig would be very, VERY big!

As farmers, we could use God's good land to grow lots of food for all of Bear Country.

And, oh yes—a word of warning for future farmers: always watch out for the bull!

There are many things to do and be. It can be hard to choose. So if you haven't found the right thing for you ...

there's no need to worry. The job for you just may not have been invented yet!

So remember, there are many different kinds of work to choose from. And with God's help, you will pick the right job, help others everyday, and have fun too!

"... Always try to do what is good for each other and for everyone else."
—1 Thessalonians 5:15

The Berenstain Bears
Get Involved

written by
Jan & Mike Berenstain

Living Lights™
A Faith Story

Brother and Sister Bear belonged to the Cub Club at the Chapel in the Woods. Preacher Brown was their leader. They did lots of fun things together. They went on picnics,

played baseball

and basketball,

sang in the chorus,
put on plays, painted
pictures of Bible stories,

and put up decorations in the
chapel at Christmastime.

But the Cub Club was about
much more than just doing fun
things.

The real purpose of the club was to help others. There was always something that needed to be done around Bear Country. Sometimes it was cleaning up the Beartown playground.

Sometimes it was bringing food to bears who couldn't get out and about.

Sometimes it was even fixing up old houses for folks who couldn't fix them up themselves.

Brother and Sister liked to be helpful. It made them feel good deep down inside. Preacher Brown explained that it was always a good thing to help those in need.

"As the Bible says," he told them, "'Whoever is kind to the needy honors God.'"

So the Cub Club went right on helping others all over Bear Country.

Little did they know that very soon their help would be truly needed indeed!

One morning at breakfast, Papa Bear was reading the weather forecast.

"Says here it will rain for the next two days," he said. "Rain, rain, and more rain!"

"Oh, dear," said Mama. "I was planning to do laundry and air it out on the line. It will have to wait."

Brother and Sister didn't pay much attention. A little rain didn't seem to be anything to get very excited about.

On the way to school, Brother and Sister noticed the sky growing very dark.

By the time they reached school, it was starting to drizzle.

Through the morning, it rained harder and harder. It rained so hard that recess was cancelled and they had a study period instead.

"Phooey on rain!" muttered Brother.

"Rain, rain, go away," recited Sister. "Come again some other day."

But the rain paid no attention. It came pouring down harder than ever.

"I think you made it worse," said Brother.

When school let out, the cubs splashed their way home through the puddles. But then they heard a car coming down the road. It was Mama. She was coming to pick them up.

"Thanks, Mama," said the cubs. "We were getting soaked!"

Back home, Papa had a fire going in the fireplace, and Mama spread their wet clothes out to dry. Brother and Sister played with Honey in front of the cozy fire.

"This rain is getting serious," said Papa. "There could be flooding along the river."

"Oh, dear!" said Mama. "That's where Uncle Ned, Aunt Min, and Cousin Fred live. I do hope they don't get flooded out."

Brother and Sister pricked up their ears. What would it mean if Cousin Fred's family got "flooded out"?

At bedtime, Brother and Sister could hear the wind howling and the rain beating against the windows. It was a little spooky, but they snuggled down under the covers and soon drifted off to sleep.

They dreamed about
rushing streams

and roaring waterfalls.

It was still raining when they woke up the next morning.

"Wow!" said Brother, pressing against the windowpane. "Look at it coming down!"

As Brother and Sister went downstairs, they heard Papa on the phone.

"Don't worry," he said. "I'll be right over!"

"Over where?" asked Mama.

"That was Preacher Brown," said Papa, getting his coat and hat. "The river is rising fast, and we'll need to get everyone out of their houses down there. We're meeting at the chapel."

"We'll all come with you," said Mama. "There'll be plenty for everyone to do."

Brother and Sister were excited. They had never been part of a rescue mission before.

At the Chapel in the Woods, bears were gathering from all over. Their cars were loaded with shovels and buckets, bundles of blankets, and boxes of food. Grizzly Gus had a load of sandbags in his truck.

Preacher Brown saw Brother, Sister, and some of the other cubs. "I want all you Cub Club members to go along with your dads and help out," he told them. "This is what the Cub Club is all about!"

"Yes, sir!" they said. They were glad to be going. And Brother and Sister especially wanted to make sure Cousin Fred was all right.

The cars drove through the storm,
down to the river.

"We're just in time," said Papa. "The
water is nearly up to the houses."

An angry river was swirling over its banks and lapping toward the houses.

"Look! There's Cousin Fred!" said Sister.

Cousin Fred, with Uncle Ned and Aunt Min, was leaning out of an upstairs window and waving.

The bears all set to work piling up sandbags and digging ditches to keep the water away from the houses. Brother, Sister, Cousin Fred, and the rest of the Cub Club joined in. They dug and dug and dug until they were cold, wet, and tired.

Then everyone drove back to the chapel to warm up, dry off, and get something to eat.

Preacher Brown's wife, along with Mama and the other moms, had soup and sandwiches ready for all those cold, wet bears. They wrapped them in dry blankets and settled them down in the chapel's pews. Miz McGrizz sat at the organ to give them a little music.

"I'm so glad you're all right!" said Mama to Uncle Ned, Aunt Min, and Cousin Fred, giving them big hugs and kisses.

Preacher Brown got up in the pulpit, opened the Bible, and started to read: "The floodgates of the heavens were opened. And rain fell on the earth ... The waters flooded the earth ..."

Sister noticed a bright light coming through the chapel windows.

"Look!" she said. "The rain is stopping, and the sun is coming out!"

"The rain had stopped falling from the sky," read Preacher Brown.

"And there's a rainbow!"
said Brother.

"I have set my rainbow in the
clouds, ... " Preacher Brown read,
and closed the Bible.

"With God's help, we are all safe and sound," said Preacher Brown. "Thanks to everyone for pitching in and helping out. I particularly want to thank our youngest helpers, the members of the Cub Club."

All the bears clapped for Brother, Sister, Cousin Fred, and the Cub Club. They had been there to help others when their help was truly needed.

The Bear family was quite proud of their handsome tree house home, and they worked hard to keep it neat and tidy. The trim was freshly painted, the front steps were scrubbed, and the windows were washed. The lawn was mowed, and the flower beds were weeded. Even the leaves of the tree were carefully trimmed and clipped.

Most of their neighbors took good care of their homes as well. The Pandas across the street were even bigger neatniks than the Bears. It seemed they were always hard at work sweeping and cleaning.

Farmer Ben's farm just down the road was always in apple-pie order too. Even his chicken coop was as neat as a pin. "A place for everything and everything in its place, that's my motto," said Farmer Ben.

The Bear family had a few neighbors whose houses were positively fancy—like Mayor Honeypot, the bear who rode around Bear Town in his long lavender limousine. His house was three stories tall and built of brick. It had a big brass knocker on the front door and statues of flamingos on the front lawn.

Even more impressive was the mansion of Squire Grizzly, the richest bear in all Bear Country. It stood on a hill surrounded by acres of lawns and gardens. Dozens of servants and gardeners took care of the place.

The Bear family was proud of their neighborhood, and they got along well with all their neighbors.

Except for the Bogg brothers.

The Bogg brothers lived in a run-down old shack not far from the Bear family's tree house—but what a difference! Their roof was caving in, and the whole place leaned to one side. There was junk all over the yard. Chickens, dogs, and cats ran everywhere. A big pig wallowed in the mud out back.

"Those Bogg brothers!" Mama would say whenever she saw them. "They're a disgrace to the neighborhood!"

"Yes," agreed Papa. "They certainly are a problem."

One bright spring morning, the Bear family was working outside, cleaning up and fixing up, when the Bogg brothers came along. They were driving their broken-down old jalopy. It made a terrific clanking racket.

As they drove past the tree house, one of the Bogg brothers spit out of the car. It narrowly missed the Bears' mailbox.

"Really!" said Mama, shocked. "Those Bogg brothers are a disgrace!"

"I agree," said Papa, getting the mail out of the mailbox. "I'm afraid they're not very good neighbors."

Papa looked through the mail and found a big yellow flier rolled up. He opened it and showed it to the rest of the family.

"Oh, boy!" said Sister and Brother. "It's like a big block party! Can we go?"
"It certainly sounds like fun," said Mama. "What do you think, Papa?"
"Everyone in town will be there," said Papa. "We ought to go too."
"Yea!" cried the cubs.

So, on Saturday morning, they all piled into the car. They had a picnic basket and folding chairs. They were looking forward to a day of fun and excitement.

But, as they drove along, the car began to make a funny sound. It started out as a Pocket-pocketa-pocketa! But it soon developed into a Pocketa-WHEEZE! Pocketa-WHEEZE!

"Oh, dear!" said Mama. "What is that awful sound the car is making?" Just then, the car made a much worse sound—a loud CLUNK! It came to a sudden halt, and the radiator cap blew off. They all climbed out, and Papa opened the hood.

"I guess it's overheated," said Papa, waving at the cloud of steam with his hat.

"Oh, no!" said Sister. "How are we going to get to the Bear Town Festival?"

"Maybe someone will stop and give us a hand," said Papa hopefully. "Look, here comes a car. Let's all wave. Maybe they will stop."

It was Mayor and Mrs. Honeypot in their long lavender limousine. They were on their way to the festival too. Their car slowed down, but it didn't stop. The mayor leaned his head out of the window.

"Sorry, we can't stop!" he said. "We're late already. I'm Master of Ceremonies today. I've got to be there on time. I'm sure someone will stop to help you."

And he pulled away with a squeal of tires.

"Hmm!" said Papa. "Maybe someone else will come along."

Soon, another car did come along. It was Squire and Lady Grizzly being driven to the festival in their big black Grizz-Royce. They slowed down too. Lady Grizzly rolled down her window.

"I'm afraid we can't stop," she said. "We don't have time. I am the judge of the flower-arranging contest. We simply must hurry."

And with that, they pulled away.

"Maybe no one is going to stop," said Sister. "Maybe we're never going to get to the festival."

"One of our neighbors is sure to stop and help us," said Mama. "After all, that's what neighbors are for."

"Yeah," said Brother. "But do *they* know that?"

A cloud of dust appeared down the road.

"Here comes someone now!" Sister said eagerly.

The dust cloud drew closer, and they could hear a clackety racket getting louder.

"Uh-oh!" said Papa, shading his eyes and peering down the road. "If that's who I think it is …"

It was!

It was the Bogg brothers.

They came clanking up in their rickety old jalopy and screeched to a halt. First one, then another, then another of the Bogg brothers came climbing out.

"Howdy!" said the first Bogg brother.

"Hello, there," said Papa.

"I'm Lem," said the first Bogg brother. "I can see yer havin' some trouble with your ve-hicle."

"Well, yes, we are," said Papa.

"Maybe we can give you a hand," said Lem.

"That would be very neighborly of you," said Papa.

"Hey, Clem! Hey, Shem!" called Lem. "Git out the rope!"

The other two Bogg brothers rooted around in the back of the jalopy and came up with a length of rope. They hitched it to the back bumper of their car and tied the other end around the front bumper of the Bears' car.

"All aboard!" said Lem. The Bear family climbed hastily back in their car. The Bogg brothers pulled away, towing the Bears' car behind them.

"Where are they taking us?" asked Mama.

Papa shrugged. "At least we're moving!"

Brother and Sister hoped the Bogg brothers weren't taking them down to their old shack. They didn't want to meet that big pig.

They soon pulled into a run-down old filling station. Someone who looked like an older version of the Bogg brothers came out.

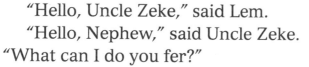

"Hello, Uncle Zeke," said Lem.

"Hello, Nephew," said Uncle Zeke. "What can I do you fer?"

"These poor folks broke down on the road," said Lem. "You reckon you can fix them up?"

"Let's take a look," said Uncle Zeke.

He looked under the car's hood, banged and clanged around, and came up with a length of burst hose.

"Radee-ator hose," he said. "Busted clean open. I should have another one of them around here somewheres."

Uncle Zeke rummaged around behind the filling station and soon came back with a radiator hose. He banged and clanged under the hood for a few more minutes.

"There," he said, wiping his hands. "Good as new. We'll top off the radee-ator, and you folks can be on your way."

"Thank you very much!" said Papa, relieved. He shook hands with Uncle Zeke and the Bogg brothers.

"Thank you!" said Mama, Brother, and Sister. Honey Bear waved.
"How much do we owe you?" asked Papa, reaching for his wallet.
"Nothin'," said Lem. "This one is on us. After all, we're neighbors."

"That's right," said Mama with a gulp. "We are. In fact, how would you neighbors like to come over to our house for dinner next week?"
Papa, Brother, and Sister all stared at Mama with their mouths open.

"That's right neighborly of you," said Lem. "Don't mind if we do! Shem's cookin' has been getting a bit tiresome—too much possum stew."

"We were on our way to the Bear Town Festival," said Papa. "Would you like to join us?"

"Sure would!" said Lem. "We ain't been to a big shindig since Grandpap's ninetieth birthday party!"

So, the Bear family drove to Bear Town with the Bogg brothers and Uncle Zeke.

They were a little late, but they hadn't missed much …
just Mayor Honeypot's welcoming speech. They all joined in
the games, rides, and contests.

When it was time for the fireworks, the Bogg brothers livened things up with some music of their own.

The next week, the Bogg brothers came over to the Bears' tree house for dinner. They wore their best clothes and got all spruced up for the occasion. They even brought a housewarming gift: a big pot of Shem's special possum stew.
It was delicious!

The Berenstain Bears'
Gossip Gang

written by
Jan & Mike Berenstain

Lizzy and Suzie were Sister Bear's best friends. They liked doing all sorts of things together. They rode bikes and jumped rope.

They played soccer outside and video games inside. They had tea parties with their dolls and stuffed animals. And sometimes they just sat around and talked.

They talked about anything and everything. They talked about TV shows and toys, about games and songs, about pets, parents, brothers and sisters, and, of course, their other friends.

"Did you hear about Queenie?" asked Lizzy. Queenie McBear was an older cub who was very popular. "I heard she has a big crush on Too-Tall Grizzly, but he has a crush on Bonnie Brown!"

"Oooh!" said the others. They were too young to have crushes yet. But they liked to talk about them.

"Did you get a load of that new cub in school?" asked Suzie. "His name is actually Teddy Bear!" The others laughed. Suzie had been a new cub not so long ago. But she didn't seem to remember.

"Well, I saw Anna Bruin the other day," said Sister, "and, you know, I think she put on some weight. She looks sort of chubby."

Lizzy and Suzie giggled.

The three friends talked for a while longer but it was soon dinnertime.
"See you!" said Sister, heading home. She liked talking to Lizzy and Suzie
about other cubs. It made her feel special and "in-the-know."

Back home, Mama and Papa were setting the table. Brother and Sister joined them.

"Do you know what Herb the mailman told me?" Papa said to Mama as he laid the silverware.

"I can't imagine," said Mama, busy putting out plates.

"He said someone saw Mayor Honeypot throwing a banana peel out his car window. Imagine—the mayor, himself, a litterbug!"

"Now, Papa," said Mama, "you know that's just gossip. You shouldn't spread stories like that."

Papa looked a little ashamed. "I guess you're right. It was just so interesting."

As they sat down to dinner, Sister had a question.

"Mama," she asked, "what's gossip?"

"Well," Mama began, "gossip is when we tell stories about others—especially stories that make them look bad. It's something we do to make ourselves feel special. It can be very hurtful.

"As the Bible says, 'gossip separates close friends.'"

"Oh," said Sister, worried. She thought maybe saying that Anna looked sort of chubby was gossip. She decided not to think about it anymore.

The next day, Sister saw Lizzy and Suzie walking ahead of her on the way to the playground. They were busy talking and didn't notice Sister coming up behind them. As Sister drew near, she overheard them talking ... about her!

"Do you know what Anna told me about Sister?" began Lizzy.

"No, what?" asked Suzie, eagerly.

"She saw Sister's spelling quiz when Teacher Jane was handing back the papers, and it was marked, '60%—very poor!'" said Lizzy.

"Wow!" said Suzie.

When Sister heard that, she stopped short. In the first place, it wasn't true. Her quiz was marked "70%—fair." That wasn't too good, but it wasn't as bad as all that.

And, in the second place, why were Lizzy and Suzie gossiping about her? They were supposed to be her best friends. She felt so bad she hid behind a tree until Lizzy and Suzie were out of sight.

As Sister came out from behind the tree, Brother Bear walked by. He was on his way to play catch with Cousin Fred.

"What on earth …?" he said. "Why are you hiding behind a tree?"

"I didn't want Lizzy and Suzie to see me," said Sister.

"Why not?" he asked.

"Because they were gossiping about me and I heard," said Sister. "I was so embarrassed!"

"I'm sorry," said Brother. "Why don't you come along with me and play catch with Fred?"
So they did.

At the playground, they started tossing the ball around. Sister could see Lizzy and Suzie on the swings, nearby. They waved and Sister waved back. Then she got angry.

"You know what I heard about Lizzy?' she called, loudly, to Fred.
"I heard that she is a big silly dope!"

"Huh?" said Fred.

"And you know what I heard about Suzie?" she yelled, even louder. "I heard that she is a funny-faced noodle-brain!"

"Sister!" said Brother.

When Lizzy and Suzie overheard Sister, they jumped off the swings and came charging over.

"Why are you saying bad things about us?" they yelled. "We thought you were our best friend!"

"That's just what I thought!" said Sister. "But I heard you gossiping about me on the way here!"

"Oh," said Lizzy. She hadn't thought about it that way. "I guess you're right. We were gossiping about you. I'm sorry!"

"Me too!" said Suzie.

Sister got over being angry right away. After all, Lizzy and Suzie were her best friends.

"That's okay," she said. "Maybe it would be better if we just didn't gossip about anyone."

Lizzy and Suzie agreed. Gossip clearly was more trouble than it was worth.

"As it says in the Bible," said Fred, who liked to memorize things, "'The tongue also is a fire.'"

"What's that supposed to mean?" said Sister.

"Just that gossiping is like playing with fire," said Fred. "You can get burnt."

"I think a game of baseball would be a lot more fun than gossip," said Brother.

"Yeah," said Sister. "Let's play!"

"I'll bet me and Fred can beat the three of you, put together," said Brother.

"You're on!" said Sister.
"Play ball!" called Fred.

Sister and her friends won.
After all, it was three against two.

Likewise, the tongue is a small part of a person's body.
But it talks big.
—James 3:5

The Berenstain Bears®

AND THE
BIGGEST
BRAG

By Mike Berenstain
Based on the characters created by
Stan & Jan Berenstain

Brother and Sister Bear were talented young cubs. They were good at all sorts of things and they worked hard at the things they were good at.

They studied hard at school.

They practiced hard at sports.

They put a lot of time and effort into art and music. They even put a lot of brainpower into playing games.

Brother and Sister were proud of their talents. They were proud of all their hard work and effort.

As a matter of fact, Brother and Sister were so proud of their talents that they sometimes bragged about them. They bragged about them mostly to each other. And it seemed to Mama and Papa they were always trying to top one another.

"I got an A in math," Brother bragged to Sister. "Well, smarty," Sister bragged back, "I got an A+!"

"I scored a goal in my soccer game," Sister bragged to Brother. "Oh, yeah?" Brother bragged back. "I scored the winning goal in my game and set up another goal with a corner kick!"

"Really!" said Mama. "Can't you two stop your endless bragging and boasting? You're both very talented cubs. Why do you have to top each other?"

"Besides," said Papa. "It's not a loving thing for a brother and sister to do. You know what the Bible says about love—'It does not envy, it does not boast, it is not proud.'"

But Brother and Sister still felt they had to be the best at everything, and they went right on with their bragging, boasting ways.

One day, after school, Brother and Sister were taking a well-deserved rest from all their hard work. They stopped at the top of a hill on their way home and lay in the soft grass looking up at the puffy white clouds. Brother and Sister imagined they saw shapes in the clouds.

"You know," said Sister, "that cloud up there looks like a big fluffy sheep."

It did, indeed, look like a fleecy white sheep grazing in a great blue meadow.

"Well," said Brother, "I think that cloud over there looks like a galloping white horse."

Sister had to admit it looked a lot like a horse. Brother's galloping white horse seemed more interesting than her fleecy white sheep. So she looked around for something better.

"I think that cloud over there looks like a dragon breathing fire and smoke," she said.

"Hmm!" said Brother. At first he didn't see it. But the more he looked, the more it did look like a dragon. He was a little annoyed. Seeing a fire-breathing dragon in a cloud was a lot better than a galloping white horse.

"Oh, yeah?" he said. "Well I think the cloud next to it looks like a knight in armor fighting the dragon." He thought some more. "And behind him there's a castle on a hill with a fair maiden who the dragon was going to eat but the knight is rescuing her." And he said to himself, *So there!*

Sister stared at the clouds, grumpily. She was not pleased that Brother had topped her dragon. Then she had an idea.

"I think those clouds look like a fleet of pirate ships shooting their cannons at a tropical island with a big fort. There's a little town with houses and church towers and swaying palm trees filled with monkeys," Sister said, and added to herself, *Top that!*

Brother was upset. How could he top a whole fleet of pirate ships and an island with swaying palm trees and monkeys? He stared at the sky, sulking. But then he noticed something.

"You know," he said, holding his hands up to the sky and looking through them, "if you look at these clouds just right ..." he squinted at them,

"... they look like the whole Solar System. The sun is in the center, then Mercury, Venus, the earth with the Moon, Mars, asteroids, Jupiter, Saturn, Neptune, Uranus, and the Kuiper Belt with Pluto, and ..."

"Oh, yeah?" shouted Sister who was mad because she had no idea what the Kuiper Belt was. "I don't think they look like the whole Solar System at all. And besides—!"

"Woah! Woah!" said a voice. "Hold your horses, up here. What's all the fussing and fretting about?"

It was Grizzly Gramps strolling by. He was out for a walk on this lovely afternoon, looking up at the puffy white clouds just like Brother and Sister.

Sister and Brother angrily explained about their "topping" contest.

"And Brother is cheating," complained Sister. "He doesn't really see any belt up there. He's just showing off!"

"Well, let me see," said Grizzly Gramps. "I'll bet I can see things up in those clouds too."

He gazed up at the clouds, rubbing his chin.

"You know," he said, "I think I see two faces in the clouds."

"Where?" said the cubs.

"Right there," said Gramps. "They look like the faces of two of the biggest, bragging-est fools I ever saw."

"Who?" asked the cubs eagerly.

"You two!" said Gramps. "None other than Brother and Sister Bear!"

"But, Gramps!" protested Brother and Sister.

"Don't 'But, Gramps!' me," said Gramps. "Admit it! Don't you two feel foolish? All this bragging and boasting about something as silly as who can see what in a cloud? Is that really something to be proud of?"

Now that they thought about it, it did seem sort of silly. What exactly were they bragging about?

"Remember what the Bible says," Gramps told them. "'Where there is strife, there is pride.'"

"We'll remember, Gramps," said the cubs.

"Now, you two come on over to my house," said Gramps. "Gran will give you milk and cookies and we'll have a nice game of checkers."

"Okay, Gramps!" said the cubs.

"I bet I win at checkers," said Brother.

"No, I'm going to win," said Sister.

"Cubs!" said Gramps.

"Oops, sorry!" said the cubs, remembering not to brag.

They walked down the hill to Gramps' and Gran's house with the beautiful white clouds floating overhead.

From: The Berenstain Bears Jobs Around Town
Activities and Questions from Brother and Sister Bear

Talk about it:

1. Why did Brother and Sister Bear decide to go out and look around Bear Country?

2. How do you know if you have found the right job for you? Where does talent and skill come from?

3. List some of the jobs that you think are most important to the community you live in. Are you interested in any of the jobs? Are these any of the same jobs Brother and Sister saw in Bear Country?

Get out and do it:

1. Talk to a pastor or children's minister about their job. Ask what you might be able to do to help them in their job. As a family, choose one of the ideas and work together to help your church leader. This may be as simple as praying for them or something more active like organizing a church-wide project such as a food drive.

From: The Berenstain Bears Ge Involved
Activities and Questions from Brother and Sister Bear

Talk about it:

1. What types of things did the Cub Club usually do for the Bear community? Does the youth group or Sunday school at your church do any of the same activities and service projects?

2. Why did many of the bears of Bear Country gather at the Chapel in the Woods?

3. Why do you think Brother and Sister are especially interested in helping out during the big rains?

Get out and do it:

1. As a family, get involved in a community or church project. Help collect food items for a food drive or blankets for a blanket collection. Organize a bake sale, and donate the funds to a local charity or to your church's service organization or mission.

2. Getting involved can be as simple as making cards for neighborhood shut-ins or people from your church that are in the hospital or a nursing home. Gather some of your friends, and make cards or write letters that give encouragement and hope to others.

From: The Berenstain Bears Love Their Neighbors
Activities and Questions from Brother and Sister Bear

Talk about it:

1. How does the Bear family feel about the Bogg brothers? Do you think they are easy to like?

2. How did the Bear family show their love for their neighbors?

3. How have you shown love for your neighbors?

Get out and do it:

1. Design a fun car with no top.

2. With your family, help a neighbor with a job like yard work.

3. Write three things you can do to help at home.

From: The Berenstain Bears Gossip Gang
Activities and Questions from Brother and Sister Bear

Talk about it:

1. Have you ever heard someone gossiping or talking about someone else? Have you ever gossiped about someone else? How did that make you feel?

2. What made Sister uncomfortable when she thought about what she had said about her friend Anna?

3. Why is gossiping wrong? If you have some news about someone that you would like to talk about, what are some options besides gossip?

4. Is it ever OK to talk about other people?

Get out and do it:

1. Be positive! Be careful what you say about others. Cut out about 20 construction-paper bees and cover a jar with brown paper to look like a hive. For one week, every time you feel like talking about someone in a gossipy way, take a bee, write a good thing about that person on it, and place it in the jar!

2. As a family, talk about someone that needs your prayers and good thoughts ... that is a good kind of "talking about someone." Then, as a family, pray together for that person, asking for God to guide and bless him.

From: The Berenstain Bears and the Biggest Brag
Activities and Questions from Brother and Sister Bear

Talk about it:

1. What exactly does it mean to "brag?" Why isn't it a nice thing for Brother and Sister Bear to do?

2. Why do you think Brother and Sister feel like they have to top each other all the time with their accomplishments? Has anyone ever done that to you? How does that make you feel?

3. What does Gramps try to teach the cubs about bragging?

Get out and do it:

1. Sit around the family dinner table and look at one another. Think of two good things about every other person at the table. Starting with the oldest person, go around the table and have each person tell their good things about him or her (for example, if the oldest person is Dad, everyone at the table needs to say two good things about Dad). Continue around the table.

2. It's OK to be proud of good things that you have done with the talents God has given you! Talk about the talents the people in your family have. Choose one of the talents and use it to help others or make someone happy. For example, if one person is good at drawing, help him make cards for people at a neighborhood nursing home.